Send Bygraves

The Old Silent
The Five Bells and Bladebone
I Am the Only Running Footman
The Deer Leap
Help the Poor Struggler
Jerusalem Inn
The Dirty Duck
The Anodyne Necklace
The Old Fox Deceiv'd
The Man with a Load of Mischief

Send Bygraves

MARTHA GRIMES

ILLUSTRATED BY

DEVIS GREBU

A PERIGEE BOOK

Perigee Books
are published by
The Putnam Publishing Group
200 Madison Avenue
New York, NY 10016

First Perigee Edition 1990
Copyright © 1989 by Martha Grimes
Illustrations copyright © 1989 by Devis Grebu

Library of Congress Cataloging-in-Publication Data

Grimes, Martha.
Send Bygraves / Martha Grimes; illustrated by Devis Grebu.
p.   cm.
I. Title.
ISBN 0-399-51646-8
PS3557.R48998S4   1990   90-7268 CIP
811'.54—dc20

Printed in the United States of America

1   2   3   4   5   6   7   8   9   10

This book is printed on acid-free paper.
∞

To Katherine Harris Grimes

wherever you are,
send Bygraves

Send Bygraves

The Beginning

I.

AT THE MANOR HOUSE (I)

He was there again today. End of lane.
Knee-deep in leaves, just by that stand of ash.
The same Burberry, furled umbrella, gun
Mirroring light. I have seen him reflected in
Shop windows, over my shoulder—commonplace,
Anonymous on park benches or under
Lampposts at the ends of passageways.
He never leaves, except for a meal or a wash.
After forty years, I have almost ceased to wonder:
Who is supplying the cash?

At first I thought (who wouldn't?) it was the folks
Wanting me out of the way. I lay in bed
Sweating it out at night with the fangs and cloaks
They called *just shadows.* No one ever comes clean
About murder or sex. They can leave you there for dead,
Tied up in an attic, or down in some ravine.

"Mum, someone's trying to kill me." "Don't be absurd,
Dear," she'd say, washing the blood from the basin.
"If we can't have a butler, how could we ever afford
To hire an assassin?"

And his turning up was not mere accident
In family snaps of hatchet-faced old hats,
All looking ghastly gray and prison-bent;
Nor there, in tiers of black-robed graduates,
Does he seem out of place, funereally
Indistinguishable from the rest.
He joined our summer outings by the sea,
The unidentified and unknown guest;
Wedding days, church socials, birthdays—he
Attended all, unasked.

I have seen him through the windows of stopped trains
In village stations, hamlets, market towns,
Cathedral cities, ends of country lanes
Like this one, where the autumn's rolling down
The hillside, and it won't be very long
Before the leaves are stacked up window-level.
Has something in his master plan gone wrong?
Or is the whole idea wearing thin?
Has death become, for both of us, less novel?
And should I ask him in?

But, no. It has to end with the police,
Getting the neighbors out of bed to make
Inquiries: *Had she many enemies?*
Ever run foul of the law? What was she last seen wearing?
They will stand in the rain with torches, they will rake
Over the gravel, measure a footprint, scrape
Blood from the sill, file a nail paring
In a paper cup. End up dragging the lake.
It will be so deadly boring.

But I won't be there to see.
Neither will he.

2.

AT THE C.I.D.

I

"Send Bygraves!" barked the Chief Inspector.
The walls went ghostlier white, the chairs
Jumped. And from the portrait the eyes of the Queen
Stared.

    The Superintendent paled. "*Bygraves?*
Man, are you daft? You know his reputation!
Scares witnesses. Hides evidence. Plants clues."

"That's as may be. But no one else can solve
This queer affair in Little Puddley, Surrey.
The lady at the manor found a body—"

"What's queer in that? We're always finding bodies.
Bygraves finds bodies no one knew were missing.
Last year: that spot of bother on Blackheath—
Bygraves kept finding bodies where no bodies
Had been reported!"

        "Still, he got his man!
Some lunatic, some Bedlamite escaped . . .
I think. Well, that's who Bygraves *said* it was.
Damn all! I can't keep tabs on all of London!
But this body in Little Puddley's different:
No one knows who it is. It comes and goes
Like old shells that the sea keeps tossing up
And dragging back. . . ."

        The Superintendent yelled:
"I'm not in the mood, old boy, for metaphysics,
Or poetry. We deal in facts, man, facts!

You're round the twist; you need your summer hols.
A week in Bournemouth, Brighton, somewhere. Now,
Get down to Little Puddley straightaway—"

"Not I!" The C.I. yelled. "Send Bygraves! Dolt!
Find Bygraves!"

        Sergeant Dolt, who had been sleeping
Hard by the door, snapped to attention. "Bygraves?
I'd get 'im sir, yes . . . only, wot's 'e look like?"

"What does he *look* like? What do you mean, you nit?"

"Now now, sir, there's no need to be abusive."
Dolt clattered up from his chair. "I never seen 'im.
'Ave you, then?"

        "Sergeant, Bygraves has been round here
Longer than you or me." The Chief Inspector
Reddened, wondered too *what did he look like?*
"Oh dash it all! Give me the phone! Bygraves!"
He shouted down the blower. *Drat the man!*
"Bygraves: I know you're there." No answer. "Bygraves!
I'm ordering you straight to Little Puddley
In Surrey." Silence. "Someone's found a body.
Bygraves?" Click. The hum of disconnection.

II

Looking towards Greenwich,
Towards that great confluence of sky and river,
Thames and Tower,
On misty mornings when Westminster rises
In this pearl-gray hour;
Had you been strolling on the Embankment then,
You would not have looked up towards Scotland Yard,
Its windows silvering in the sun,
And thought: *Murder is abroad.*
No, you would not have known
The blind man coming towards you in these waves
Of Londoners, his white stick tapping
The ground like a divining rod, is looking
Over his shoulder at you.

Was it Bygraves?

3.

LODGINGS

These are Bygraves' rooms.
Do not touch a thing.
Stuff out of his pockets—
Notebook, change, key ring.
Careful. If he comes
Back and finds us at it . . .
Do not think about it.
Do not touch a thing.

Notice how the floor
Tilts. And notice there
Where the wallpaper
Seems to conceal a door.
Set that table straight;
Leave those chairs around it.
Fool! That paperweight—
Put it where you found it.

See your face dissolving
In his wardrobe mirror,
Like a face in water;
See its surface moving.
Do not touch the glass!
Do not be alarmed.
I have heard that others
Have escaped unharmed.

Stay back from those windows!
Wipe that knob you touched!
Cling to walls and shadows.
Fool! Put out that match!
What? You thought you heard
A key turn in the lock?
Quiet. Not a word.
Quick. Out the back.

4.

THE REGULARS
AT THE *BELL AND ANCHOR*,
LITTLE PUDDLEY, SURREY

We're a decent lot. We cause no trouble.
(That spot of bother with the poisoned dogs
At Smythe-Montcrieff's? We'd nothing to do with that!)
You standing, Sergeant? Ah, thank you, I'll have a Double
Diamond. Jameson on the side. That fog's
Thick as pea soup ihnit? I'll tell you flat:
We don't much like the Yard nosing about
In Little Puddley. Keep ourselves to ourselves,
We do. We've nothing to hide. We're a decent lot.

We don't know—right, mates?—nothing about no murder.
We come to the Bell for a friendly pint and a game—
Shove-penny, a bit of darts, it's all the same.
Only listen: there's hugger-mugger up at that manor.
Ain't that right, Trev? Trevor was gardener
For thirty years. But now the help won't stay.
There's Fiona Rugg was cook there all these years;
The one-eyed chauffeur, he quit too; and Scroggs,
Scullery girl, they say she left in tears.

We've heard of this chap, Bygraves. There's a strange one.
Dihn't he find them bodies on Blackheath?
No one knew who they was nor where they came from?
You'd think he'd spun them up out of thin air.
You standing again? Yes, thanks; I'll have a Guinness.
I'll tell you straight, it fair gives me the creeps
To think of fog out there and Bygraves in it.
Look there! Whose face was that against the window?
Another round, Mrs. Peach! This bloody fog.

I'd not go out on a night like this, no, sir.
Except to the Bell, of course, not with this fog;
Not with this wind, screeching across the moor.
Blind Willie says he hears them dogs. That's blather,
I say. But there's strange doings in Little Pud.
Like the things that's happened to Whipsnade's ladylove
(All artsy-tartsy she is with her foreign ways!).
What? You ain't heard of that? Let's have another—
Mrs. Peach! Mrs. Peach! Two pints, please, of best bitter.

Life's a mug's game, only joy for crooks and saints.
Trying to puzzle it out—now, that's where the trouble starts.
Here at the Bell and Anchor we've no complaints.
Life's a mug's game. Stick to your pints and darts.

5.

AT THE LODGE

Major Snively is cleaning his guns.
Hounds sprawl like logs
Across the hearth. Ever since
That wretched business of the poisoned dogs
He's had them in. Snively listens hard:
What noise came from the yard?
Fog like a curtain. Snively checks the locks.
Has he forgotten anything?
Fingerprints wiped clean; the clocks
Turned back; the chairs upended;
The broken statue of Eros mended.

Snively remembers:
Fear rises in him like a flight of birds.
The shout. The sharp report.
The hound returning with the bloodstained glove.
Over the mantel gleam the polished swords
Of the old regiment. His orderly
White-turbaned and gold-toothed. Sahib. Sahib.
Pink gin beneath the palms. The camel bells.
Snively mops his brow; he's through.
This is the end of him.
His dreams are bad. Blood falls like dew.

What was that tapping on the pane?
That scraping on the gravel?
Snively stumbles to the window:
The rag-and-bone man back again!
What is he looking for?
Snively wonders if
The bloodstained glove is buried deep enough.
That Scotland Yard lot's given him no peace,
And that chap Bygraves seemed too curious.
What noise was that? Whose footstep on the terrace?

6.

AT THE MANOR HOUSE (II)

Scroggs found him first by the statue of Eros,
Impossible to mistake
The man (the same Burberry, gun)
Who watched me from the ends of lanes;
And yet by morning he was gone.
All day we searched the grounds, the woods.
I remember the way the rooks
Cawed in the treetops. Sinister, that.
Rugg, the cook, took fright and packed.
Next day we found him by the lake.

We thought it odd. The chauffeur, Quickly,
Stumbled on him three days later
Face down in the kitchen garden.
Then by evening, he was gone,
The cabbage patch completely wrecked.
Vanished, nothing left
Except his glove and trilby hat.
Now Scroggs has gone, and Rugg and Quickly.
Well, what did I expect?
You can't keep servants after that.

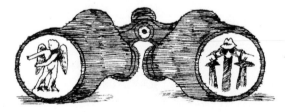

I wait alone, except for Sneed,
Whom I distrust. All day I sweep
Binoculars across the lawn.
The formal garden's gone to seed.
The locals stand about ten-deep.
I've picked out Snively, Whipsnade, Crumb,
Having a turn round the estate.
What does it mean? I still can't shake
The feeling that I'm being watched.
They've called the Yard in much too late.
The case will, in the end, be botched.

7.

A NOTE FROM BYGRAVES FOUND
UNDER A MALT VINEGAR JUG

The dark suspicions of a winter's night:
The missing hands of clocks.
The poisoned chocolates in the heart-shaped box.

8.

ROSE COTTAGE

Miss Ivers serves the Chivers marmalade
With trembling hands. Miss Ivers is nervous.
Miss Ivers is in love with Dr. Whipsnade,

Engaged to Lady Madrigal du Bois,
Pale, blonde, and vaguely foreign, whom he saved
From being trampled underneath her horse.

The reins were cut. But who would have believed
The girl had enemies? There was that awful
Episode in Creeper's Wood, that brief

Incident at Snively's with the rifle.
A good thing Whipsnade found the arsenic
Traces in the cocoa and the trifle.

Poor Madrigal. Thin, faded, turned to drink,
Imagining her body lying on
Dredcrumble Moor, or buried in a trunk.

"More marmalade, my dear? Another scone?"
Miss Ivers asks. Her rooms are cold and poor.
Miss Ivers has lived all her life alone

Watching the fog roll off Dredcrumble Moor,
Thick and close and certain as old age.
What will she do now Scotland Yard is here?

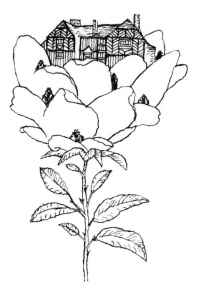

Who walked behind her from the vicarage?
Who tampered with her lock? Who took her key?
Who left the knifemark on the window ledge?

"More marmalade, my dear? Are you unwell?"
"It tastes a bit bitter," says Madrigal.

9.

P.C. FEATHERS AT THE GEORGE HOTEL

They've cornered Feathers at the George Hotel:
There's Keepyhole, the butcher; there's Miss Crumb,
The Little Pud postmistress; there's Blind Willie,
Village Teiresias; there's poor Tom Spratt,
Who at the age of fifteen was struck dumb
By lightning in a field of cows.

                                "Well, Feathers,

Whose body is it, then?"

                        "Nobody knows."
"Well, what's the Scotland Yard lot doing, then?"
Asks Keepyhole. "I hear it comes and goes
Like Rose's virtue. There, love, another round!"
Giggles. More beer. The judgment of Miss Crumb:
"You'll not laugh when we're throttled in our sleep.

I don't much fancy lying in a heap
In Creeper's Wood." Silence while this sinks in.
Tom grins and drools a bit and bangs for gin.
Blind Willie lays his finger by his nose.
Keepyhole says: "This Bygraves chap, you've seen him,
Feathers. What's he like?"

                  "*I've* never seen him.
Nobody's seen him—only at a distance:
On country roads, down lanes, across the park,
Or in a stand of trees, or after dark,
If you see torchlight show window to window,
That's Bygraves." No one speaks. "A funny thing, though,
The lanes are darker once Bygraves has been there;
The house is emptier when Bygraves leaves it;
The woods are colder when Bygraves has walked there."

They all stare at the fire. Flames shoot. Logs spark.
Keepyhole pounds for beer. Spratt looks slack-mouthed.
Miss Crumb eats Bovril crisps. "But he's in charge;
How's he give you orders?"

"Writes us notes."

"He writes you *notes?*"

"Yes, notes."

"What kind of notes?"

"Telling us to go here or to go there,
To look for this or that. And listen close—
We always find what Bygraves says we'll find:
Letters, a ticket stub, a broken locket,
Faded snapshot, bit of colored glass,
Jar of marmalade—"

           "A poisoned dog!"
Blind Willie winks his boiled-egg eye and cackles.
"Get on with ye!" cries Feathers. "That's all blather."
"I heard 'em!" shouts Blind Willie. "Oh, I heard 'em!
Streamin' across Dredcrumble Moor o' nights,
Howlin' and scratchin' at the trees. 'Twas awful!"
"Oh, bosh!" says Crumb. "It's all an old wives' tale!
"It's daft."

      "It's daft."

        "It's daft."

          "It's even dafter
Than poor Tom Spratt. Hey, Tom?"

             Tom smiles and slobbers.

IO.

THE CLUE IN THE BOG

Dredcrumble Moor! Isn't that where
Young Brian Jumpers wandered off
Without a word? Where Nellie Clough
Took the shortcut to the fair
And disappeared? Where Lady Breedlove
Vanished with her chestnut mare?

Rain freezes on the heather. Fog
Closes like a glove. Police
Shine their torches. The C.I.D.'s
Billingsgate stares at the bog.
The severed hand he thinks he sees
Is just a glove caught on a log.

Beneath it is a torn snapshot,
Poorly focused, of a man
In trilby hat, dark glasses, raincoat.
Billingsgate hands round the snap
Later in the Bell and Anchor:
"Any of you lot know this chap?"

They all deny it in the boozer.
Raincoat, glasses, trilby hat . . .
Doesn't that description fit
The body found up at the manor?
Wait a tick! This chap was at
The bookstall reading *Chips and Whizzer*. . . .

What a bloody awful case.
Billingsgate picks at his mutton,
Wishes he could find Bygraves,
Wishes he were home at Luton.
Now he gets some dreadful news:
Lady Madrigal du Bois
Collapsed at noon playing badminton.

II.

ABOUT TOM SPRATT

We wish that he would stop at home
Instead of wandering the streets
Accosting everyone he meets
And babbling nonsense, but that's Tom.

He's always setting off alarms
And getting out the fire brigade,
Or pouring ale on someone's head
Down at the Bell or Chairman's Arms.

Because he lolls and lollygags,
Because he drops his trousers down,
Because he wears his shirts backwards,
No one suspects he killed the dogs—

And yet, who knows what passions seethe
In Tom Spratt's breast for Madrigal
(Engaged to Whipsnade, secretly
In love with Geoffrey Smythe-Montcrieff,

That huntsman with his pack of hounds,
Who rides in pinks and sounds his horn).
Tom hunkers down on frosty morns
In thickets while they do their rounds,

Thinking his evil, evil thoughts,
Rolling his eyeballs back to whites.
He haunts Dredcrumble Moor o' nights
And plots, and plots, and plots, and plots—

He'll fall into the lake and drown,
Or be sucked down by quicksand, that's
The way it ends with idiots.
There's one of them in every town.

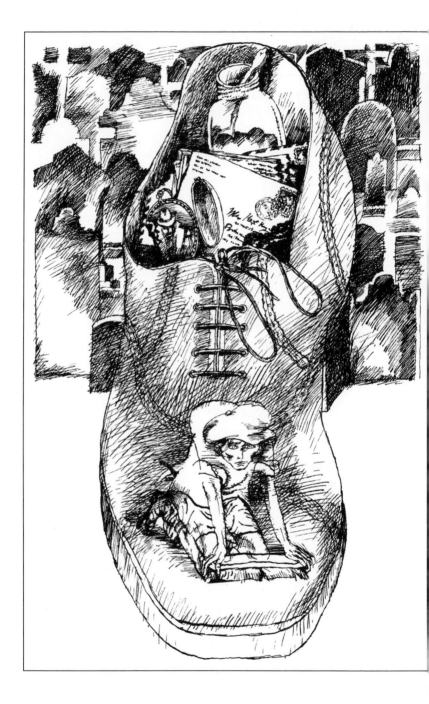

12.

THE SAD (BUT REALISTIC) TALE
OF BRIAN JUMPERS

Little Brian Jumpers, the main waif in
Little Puddley, pale and sad and sickly,
Little threadbare jacket out at elbow,
Face all tear-streaked, socks around his ankles,
Worked all day at shining shoes and sweeping
Chimneys, blacking things that needed blacking:
Bottles, tar pits, coal cellars, macadam.

Little Brian Jumpers did the awful
Jobs nobody wanted—scrubbing gravestones,
Cleaning loos—all that was wretched, nasty,
Only asking for his tiny pittance.
(No one paid him in the decimal system,
Only in old currency like shillings,
Sixpence, tuppence, bobs, and ha'pennies,
He was saving for his operation.)

Little Brian Jumpers had a boxful
Of treasures found down wells or up in chimneys,
Letters rescued from some burning embers,
Jar of marmalade, a broken locket,
Bloodstained glove he'd found by an old gravestone—
Little Brian knew his solemn duty
Was to take this lot to the police.
Brian walked all night across the moor, but . . .
Little Brian Jumpers never made it.

13.

THE BUDGIE CLUE

Down on the badminton court
They are reviving Madrigal.
Miss Ivers is hysterical;
Whipsnade rubs her ankles while
Snively makes her drink some port.
(Poor Madrigal. It's rather vile

To have one's life hang by a thread,
To have to check the post for bombs,
To keep a pistol by one's bed,
To keep jumping at every sound,
To keep back from the cliff's sheer edge
To keep from getting shoved or drowned.)

Billingsgate is in the kitchen
With Demelda Sly, the cook:
"What did your mistress have for luncheon?"
"Beef, olives, and spotted dick
For afters." "Did she ever mention
Anyone about who looked

Anyway the least suspicious?"
"Just Miss Crumb brought up the post,
And Keepyhole brought round the roast,
And Tom Spratt popped up in the bushes,
And Mr. Plum, who happened past—
He's a salesman, selling budgies."

The kettle whistles on the hob.
"Mr. Plum? And who is *he*?"
"Don't rightly know; he wore a trilby
Hat and raincoat. Quite the nob
Was Mr. Plum. I made some tea
And bought a budgie for ten bob."

A clue. The caged budgerigar
Puts Billingsgate in mind of—what?
Badminton birds! A poisoned dart
Stuck in the feathers! Fiendish plot!
Where's Bygraves? wonders Billingsgate.
I'll get the truth out of this lot!

Meanwhile, Ivers, Whipsnade, Snively
Have been joined by Keepyhole,
Miss Crumb, Tom Spratt and Blind Willie,
And the regulars from the Bell.
Is one of them our "Mr. Plum"?
They all look off. It's hard to tell.

Whipsnade shouts: "Enough's enough!"
(What's wrong with Whipsnade?) "We've our rights!
You London chaps have cut up rough!
I'll have your badge! And Bygraves, what's
He bloody up to?" Billingsgate,
Sick of Whipsnade, says, "Get stuffed."

14.

AT THE COBWEB TEAROOMS

Fiona Rugg and Millie Scroggs
Stop for their elevenses
In the Cobweb Tearooms, run
By Mrs. Kingston-Biggs, poor thing,
Whom fortune forced into the trade,
Who once kept servants by the score—
But that's another story. Now
She serves up set teas and gâteaux.

You'd never know that Rugg and Scroggs,
So friendly-like they seem, quite loathe
One another. Both of them are
In love with Quickly, the chauffeur,
Who's made rash promises to both.
But worse to come: Fiona's sure
That Millie found her locket lying
By the broken statue of Eros.

And Millie knows Fiona has
The negatives of dirty pictures
Whipsnade took in surgery
That day she weakened. Dreadful man!
You can't trust no one nowadays!
To think he's got the sauce to marry
Lady Madrigal du Bois!
Millie searches out the pills

She stole from Whipsnade's shelf, and when
Fiona leaves to freshen up,
She drops them in Fiona's cup.
That should take care of you, my girl!
Fiona's back and watching; while
Millie chats with Kingston-Biggs,
Fiona sprinkles something vile
On Millie's chocolate gâteaux.

An hour later, feeling sickly,
Each is sure she'll be the one
To scarper off and marry Quickly.

15.

IN SURGERY

Whipsnade puts the poison up,
Draws the curtains, wipes the knife,
Burns some papers in his safe.
Whipsnade: such a decent chap!
Who would think his plans were for
Getting rid of Smythe-Montcrieff?
Now he leaves and locks the door,

Throws the scalpel and the gun
In the stream by the Old Mill.
Nothing's left now to be done:
Madrigal has signed her will.
Whipsnade starts. The curtains billow.
What gloved hand lay on the sill?

        (This is just one more subplot
        To confuse the reader, who's
        Not the fool some think he is.
        Whipsnade is that handsome, silky-
        Talking, hero-type that's flat
        Out for jewels, or sex, or money.
        It was Whipsnade drugged her cocoa,
        Cut her reins. But we knew that.)

16.

AT THE POST OFFICE STORES

Miss Crumb, startled by the bell,
Stuffs the bloodstained glove
Dug up from Major Snively's roses
In the mail receptacle.

Who is this stranger in the raincoat,
Dark glasses, and trilby hat?
Is he the salesman from Godalming?
The road-works man from Aldershot?

Marmaduke, her ginger cat,
A red bandanna round its neck,
Claws the mahogany countertop,
Flings itself upon the floor,

Sniffs the mail receptacle,
Roots through letters, cards, and parcels,
Finds the glove and drags it over
To the stranger in the balaclava.

Marmaduke
Is a nasty bit of work.

17.

LADY WHITSUN DIED

Lady Whitsun died
Holding a *carte-de-visite*
Of a man in a landscape. Was it
Truly him in the mist
Where hounds had raised a scent
By Snuffling Copse? Just
As he looked in this picture, dressed
In a raincoat and trilby hat,
Handsome, his face in shadow,
Behind him, the long meadow.

Why had he come back *now*,
After she thought him dead?
How could she face it, how
Explain to police the spreading
Stain on the Axminster carpet?
Or what's in the potting shed?
Lady Whitsun died
Over her pot of tea
And biscuits and Banbury
Tarts and cyanide.

Wearing her blue peignoir
And clutching to her breast some gray
Letters, ribbon-tied,
Lady Whitsun died.
Weeping, she downed the lot;
The cup, the biscuit unbitten
Dropped from her hand to the floor.
Fog slipped under her door
Like the letter she never got:
Thin, gray, cold, unwritten.

The Middle

18.

MURDERACROSTIC

What's happened to the Puddley pack?
How could it be they've disappeared
And not a horn to call them back
Through copse and comb? It's as we've feared:
Something's afoot. No one will shout

A view hallo, the whip's cap up—
Luther, Lisper, Lark, and Luv,
Lurcher leading, steady at banks,

Throwing tongue near Snuffling Copse,
Hounds that used to feather out
Into coverts, rolling up
Scent like reels of silk. Now there's

Nothing but silence. Hunter, horn
Over a fly country have flown.
Where has it gone, the best of the fun?

19.

MURDERCONCRETE

What's all this, now? 'ello, 'ello, 'ello, 'ello, The Eternal Question

20.

MURDERANAPHORA

The spectre walks Dredcrumble Moor;
The spectre drifts above the bog;
The spectre floats like frost smoke where
The spectre merges with the fog.
The spectre wanders Crackclaw Heath;
The spectre troubles Fretfall Close;
The spectre moans. What awful death
The spectre suffered, no one knows.
The spectre glides through rain and rime;
The spectre follows kings and fools;
The spectre comes to all in time.

The spectre! How you dread to see
The spectre here, and in dark pools
The spectre mirrored endlessly.

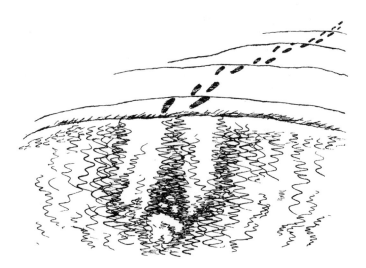

21.

MURDERSONNET

There's something funny in the potting shed
Besides the smell of damp earth and dead roses—
The windows locked, the door warped shut—it poses
A question of what happened here. What bled
This trail from floor to sill to flower bed?
What scarred the footpath here? What left these traces
Of something dragged across the shasta daisies?
This shrubbery disturbed? These lupins dead?

Old Trev (the gardener), they say, went mad
From witnessing too many wills. He hides
Behind the peonies and stares in windows.
And where's Lord Whitsun? Something here betides
An ominous outcome—all those petunias
Trampled, and this dreadnought in the zinnias.

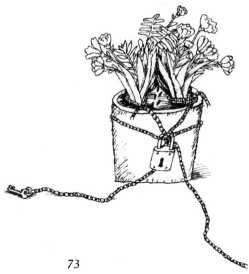

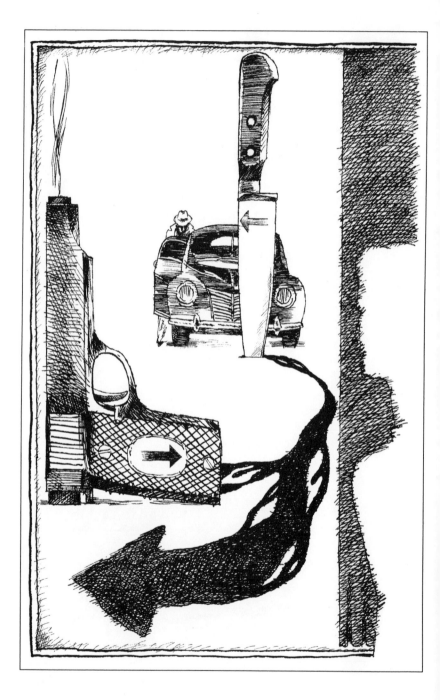

22.

MURDERPANTOUM

Down the wrong paths to the wrong answers lie
Clues that are planted to mislead the eye.
On Spectre Hill, a coach is passing by.
It will stop in your courtyard presently.

Clues that are planted to mislead the eye:
The gun, the knife, the bloodstain on the floor.
It will stop in your courtyard presently,
The driver will step down and try your door.

The gun, the knife, the bloodstain on the floor,
They are not what they seem to be at first.
The driver will step down and try your door.
As in an ending cleverly reversed,

They are not what they seem to be at first.
In silence sometimes lies the only hope.
As in an ending cleverly reversed,
Beware. Be still. Be patient. Let him grope.

In silence sometimes lies the only hope.
Some say there is an answer in the sky.
Beware. Be still. Be patient. Let him grope
Down the wrong paths to the wrong answers. Lie.

The End

23.

WHY DON'T WE KILL THEM OFF
AND BE DONE WITH IT?

Bobby and Bunch
(The Honorable Smeel-Carruthers twins,
And staples of the Puddley social scene)
Are always turning up at lunch,
Or at hunt breakfasts wearing hacking jackets,
Or suddenly appearing on
The terrace swinging tennis racquets.

Bobby and Bunch
(Brother and sister—they've the same
Blue eyes and flaxen hair and ruddy cheeks)
Say things like "Topping game!"
Or "Stone the crows!" or "Sticky wicket!" or
"I say, you *are* a brick!"
Or else, "We're off to London Wednesday week."

They drink a lot of sherry, tie their sweaters
Around their necks and drive an open car.
And when it rains they stay at Stubbings
(The family seat), or else go slumming
Down at the Bell. One never finds them far
From moneyed uncles, cream teas, and croquet.
Their hobby is brass rubbings.

No matter what
Garrotings, knifings, poisonings, or heads
Stashed in hat boxes under beds
Turn up, or torsos tossed in trunks,
Walks running red with blood, air thick with menace—
Bobby and Bunch
Will unaccountably be playing tennis.

Why must it be these two who find
Lady Whitsun dead? Poor Billingsgate
Is stuck with them: "Now, Mr. Smeel-Carruthers,
And Miss—you didn't touch
Anything, did you?" "Heavens, no!"
Says Bunch. "At least not much,"
Says Bobby, "nothing but the letters—

"We tossed those in the grate. And scrubbed the stain
Out of the Axminster. And then the cup—
You know—the tea things needed washing up
Straightaway. I had some port and read
A bit whilst Bunch was in the potting shed."

"The potting shed!"
(Poor Billingsgate.) "What were you doing *there*?"
"Just having a look round. There's heaps
Of arsenic and prussic acid, blood
Splashed all about. And then the gardener—"
"Gardener?" "Yes. Dressed in a queer old coat
And balaclava. Well, he's not our sort
At all. Oh, Bobby, Bobby!
Lord Whitsun's got a smashing tennis court!"

24.

INTIMATIONS

Rain. Wind. Fog
Like gas above the ground
In Spoorscar Cemetery,
Where the heaped headstones
Drown in leaves and lichen,
Weed-bound, moss-begotten,
Where someone waits alone
Hidden in the bracken.

Wind. Fog. Rain
After evensong
Veils the path the verger
Lately crept along;
Where the cry of nightjars
Over Crackclaw Heath
Haunts the humpbacked bridge,
Someone waits beneath.

Fog. Rain. Wind
Rattles the box laurel,
Mutes the sound of footsteps
Coming on the gravel;
Something in the air,
Something like an ax—
The sharp question: *Who's there?*
The whispered answer: *Don't look back.*

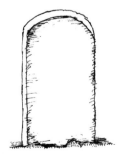

25.

COLONEL BYWATERS TO HIS BUTLER

Tell me, Riddley:
What is that drink spilt on the rug, that stain
Running down the wall, the furniture
All anyhow, the draperies in shreds?
And isn't this old Snively's walking stick?
Where is he, then? I didn't see his Bentley.

Damn all, Riddley!
What's been going on? I turn my back,
Go off for a week's shooting up in Scree—
Bring in that brace of pheasant, there's a good chap—
And then come back to this. I see
You've left a dead cat lying in the garden.
You try my patience, Riddley. Why's the post

Been messed about this way upon the salver?
Bills, bills, more bills. . . . I see the hunt's to meet
Down at the Barley Mow. That Smythe-Montcrieff
Has shown good sport. But too much wire
On Crackclaw Heath. It's all touts, tarts, and farmers,
Anyone in for a fiver. What's this, then?

Who brought this ax in from the shed? And why's
My pistol missing from its case? Riddley,
Have you been at the port again? Lady
Eiderdown requests my presence at
One of her dreadful lawn parties. Speaking
Of lawns, look there. Look! Who's that on the path
In dreadnought and dark glasses? Riddley? Riddley!

Wake up, man! Find my shirt studs. Draw the bath.

26.

WHISTLEBY'S SONG

Whistleby,
The Little Pud poet laureate,
Strikes out across the heath,
Hair like milkweed, shirt undone,
Under his arm a slim volume
Of poetry. Whistleby
Stumbles on a log, strangles
On a vine, is within an ace
Of being sucked down in Crackclaw Bog.
Whistleby's only alive by the grace
Of God or the Queen. Poor sod.

Whistleby's thoughts scatter like leaves:
Why has he come? What dark design
Has forced him out-of-doors, gone off
And left his linen on the line?
Or left the kettle on the hob?
Or left that sonnet someone wanted?
Or left a debt of twenty bob?
Or left the sherry undecanted?
Or left the post without a stamp?
Or left the cat up in a tree?
Or left the dog out in the damp?

Whistleby stops to write an ode
On the humpbacked bridge. Dear God!
The very stones are weeping blood.
What is that floating downstream, snarled
Amongst the rocks? A bundle of
Letters and a pearl-gray glove?
Just as he plucks them out he sees
Racing across Crackclaw Heath
A motorcyclist—leather boots,
Trilby, dark glasses, dreadnought
Flashing in and out of sight
Like a dark and tangled thought.

Whistleby's life is one long trial
Full of thickets, snares and traps,
Dangerous corners turned, unwise
Actions and precipitate
Accidents—scrapes, lunges, falls,
Headlong crashes into walls,
Lethal potions, mortal coils
He can't shake off—

> And *now* he'll go
> Straight to police. We know whose plate
> This lot will land on. Billingsgate
> Might as well shake down stars from a tree
> As try to shake sense out of Whistleby.

27.

A NOTE FROM BYGRAVES
TO CONSTABLE FEATHERS
FOUND FLOATING IN THE DUCK POND
BY TWO CHILDREN

Constable Feathers, I see
Nothing unusual here:
The tradespeople, the gentry,
The servants, the village lout—
All of the villagers out
To murder one another
In typical English fashion.
I wander through the fog,
Pondering the red herrings:
The bloodstained glove, the dogs,
The marmalade, the locket—
Laid on to cover up
The body at the manor,

Gone, last seen wearing
Trilby or balaclava.
I stroll through the typical High Street's
Tangle of shops and pubs
In dark glasses, Burberry,
Unrecognizable
In my corner of the Bell.
In Boots and the newsagent
I have been taken for
A dustman, the Prince Regent,
Or someone with something to sell.

Feathers, it is midnight.
Shadows throng my room.
Ice forms in the puddles.
I scratch this out by lamplight.
I wonder sometimes while
Standing in copse or wood,
Watching from ends of lanes:
Will murder go out of style?
Will the halls of the C.I.D.
Ring like singing bone,
Echo hollowly
With no one to carry on?
Will crime be shot of me?
Will England be gone?

Rubbish, Feathers! Forget it!
I think it is time to gather
All of the suspects together.
Attached is a letter. Don't let it
Fall into the wrong hands.

28.

AT THE MANOR HOUSE (III)

We have assembled in the library.
Whipsnade's here, and Snively's come;
Keepyhole, Tom Spratt, Blind Willie,
Madrigal, Miss Ivers. Crumb
Hands round cakes and salted almonds.
Sneed, the butler, pours the sherry.

We've chatted, smoked awhile, got bored
With one another rather quickly.
The little warnings we've ignored:
That pool of blood that's spreading thickly;
The strangled cries we overheard—
We'll deal with those directly

After tea. I've rung for Sneed,
Who does not come, who, I'm afraid,
No longer answers every need.
The fire's unlit; the cloth's unlaid;
And no one's seen the upstairs maid
For ages. We have all agreed

Something is wrong. Doors creak. Panes rattle.
Leaves have piled up in the passage;
Light fades from the hills and ridges;
Drifts of snow have come to settle
On the sills and window ledges.
All of us have read your letter:

One of us tampered with his food.
One of us struck him on the path.
One of us lured him to the wood.
One of us drowned him in his bath.
One of us shot him on the road.
One of us strangled him in wrath.

Inspector Bygraves, in the dark
We watch you smoking by the gate;
In the environs of the park
There is nothing to do but wait.
Will you step from the shadowed walk
And turn, and strike, and leave no mark?

29.

THE UNFORTUNATE END OF DETECTIVE SERGEANT BILLINGSGATE, CHRONICLED IN A NOTE TO CHIEF INSPECTOR BYGRAVES, AND FOUND IN THE PLEASANCE OF THE MANOR HOUSE

Sir:
I have questioned the lot
Down at the Bell and Anchor,
The Chairman's Arms and the George.
Something has come to light:
This stranger hereabouts
Some say is a salesman, some,
A rag-and-bone man of sorts
Was last observed in the fog
At the end of Beggar's Alley,

Wearing a trilby hat
(Some say a balaclava),
Burberry and rolled umbrella.
Odd. The description fits
The body at the manor.

Sir:
I begin to see
What has been going on.
Perhaps we have stumbled across
Some quintessential crime
Of which all others are less
Than shadowy replicas.
(Forgive me for putting it thus
Philosophically—
You came up through the ranks and distrust,
I suppose, a Cambridge degree.)
I stroll through the gardens and lanes
Where rumors are thick as vines,
Riddles are carved on walls,
Secrets are struck in stones.
Here where the manor house
Rises unreally,
Only the wind has a voice;
Fog veils the fields. Silence
Is like a wall. Murder
Is not what it used to be.

I am leaving my report
Here on this bench by the lake
With my badge and identity card.
Say good-bye to my wife and my mates
On the force. Say, if you will,
I was walking alone on the moor,
Or say I was working too hard,
Or say I was troubled of late.
But say I was true to the Yard.
Sir: I have always been
Your servant,

Billingsgate.

30.

THE BYGRAVES SESTINA

That chap on the corner smoking a fag is Bygraves,
Isn't it? Was it at Harrogate
Last winter when you saw him, or at Bury
Saint Edmunds, Michaelmas? Or all those times
In London's goblin lanes or ends of empty
Alleys when you thought you were alone?

A milky light glows in the George. A lone
Dog rattles the dustbins. Was it Bygraves
Who watched you where the milk-float stopped to empty
Pint bottles by the Bell and Anchor's gate?
Or in the newsagent's reading the *Times*,
In dark glasses, trilby hat, Burberry?

The milk-float leaves. The dog trots off to bury
His rag and bone. Fog strands you here alone
By Spoorscar Cemetery. There are times
Trees, lampposts, shadows take the shape of Bygraves—
Even this beggar standing by the lych-gate,
In balaclava, raincoat, pockets empty.

You hurry by his cup of sorrows, empty-
Handed, save for what you came to bury:
The glove, the *carte-de-visite*—(Did the gate
Click shut?) You see, along the path, the lone
Gravedigger, leaning on his shovel. (Bygraves
Will never think to search these graves in time.)

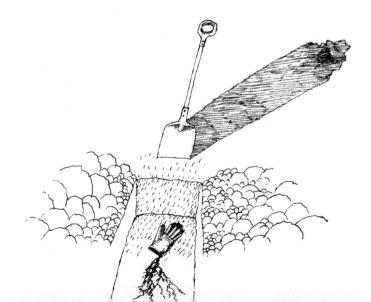

You will be bound for London in the meantime,
Far from Little Puddley's bleak and empty
Moors and fens and marshes—far from Bygraves.
You find the station, buy your ticket, bury
Your face behind the *Puddley Post.* A lone
Porter stacks the mailbags by the gate.

An hour to wait. The Bell has locked its gate.
The barmaid in the Barley Mow calls, "Time,
Please, gentlemen." On the High Street alone,
You try the Chairman's Arms, the George. Both empty.
But on the road, that chap in the Burberry,
Smoking the fag. Surely, it must be Bygraves.

The past is dead and buried. It is time
You go to meet him, hand outstretched. "Bygraves!"
A gate creaks in the wind. The road is empty.

31.

A NOTE FROM BYGRAVES BLOWN ACROSS DREDCRUMBLE MOOR AND INTO YOUR HANDS

Mystery. It's all the same:
Questions without end or aim.

What will lead us to the dead?
Footprints in the flower bed.

What appeals were made too late?
Sift the ashes in the grate.

What was fatal in the mug?
Pick the fragments from the rug.

What has tolled the final knell?
Find the sexton and the bell.

What heart had become too fond?
Cast the net across the pond.

What act was misunderstood?
Take the footpath to the wood.

What mind had succumbed to grief?
Search the rocks beneath the cliff.

What was buried in the sand?
Shine the lantern down the strand.

Clues that lie as scattered as
The blown leaves across our paths.

Silence, speak. Wind, unwind.
Everything will be explained.

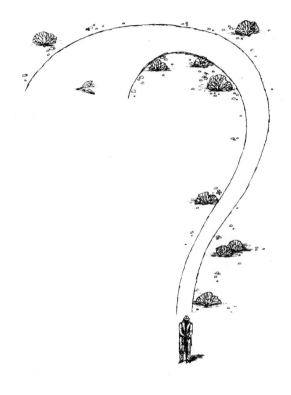

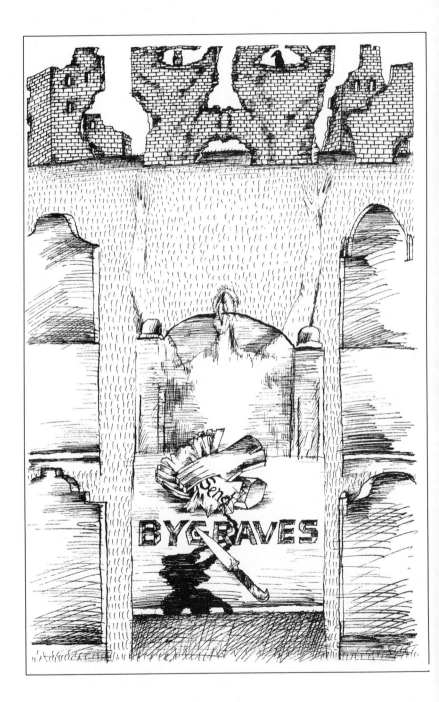

Epilogue

UNTITLED PARCHMENT FOUND AMONG
THE RUINS OF CRUNCHLEY ABBEY,
NR. MORDANT-IN-MARSH, SURREY

There was a house across the moor.
There was a house. There is no more.
There is a lady chapel where
A knight lies by his lady fair,
Their marble likenesses the bare
Memory of who they were.

There is a tale. It goes like this:
That she, for his unfaithfulness,
Killed him with a poisoned kiss.
Now every night in her distress
She must rise up from her stone dress
And walk the moor, till she confess.

So few there are in earth or heaven
To whom the power to shrive is given,
Across the moor by conscience driven,
Three hundred years she's walked unshriven;
Her only friends are owl and raven,
And morning light, her only haven.

The rattle of October leaves
Covers their twin effigies.
A wind blows through the nave and moves
The message in her marble gloves,
A scrap of paper that she saves
In hopes you'll find it:

MARTHA GRIMES lives in Washington, D.C. She is the author of ten novels, including the best-selling *The Five Bells and Bladebone* and *The Old Silent*.

DEVIS GREBU's work has appeared in magazines, books, and exhibitions all over the world, including the recent book *Devis Grebu: Through an Artist's Eye*. He lives in Ossining, New York.